Welcome to The GROW & READ Early Reader Program!

The GROW & READ book program was developed under the supervision of reading specialists to develop kids' reading skills while emphasizing the delight of storytelling. The series was created to help children enjoy learning to read and is perfect for shared reading and reading aloud.

These GROW & READ levels will help you choose the best book for every reader.

GROW & READ
Developing Confidence for Success in Reading

GROW & READ 1

Level 1: Starting to Read (Preschool-Grade 1) Simple sentences and easy sight words for growing confidence

GROW & READ 2

Level 2: Reading with Help (Grades 1-2) Longer text, problem solving and growing vocabulary

GROW & READ 3

Level 3: Reading Independently (Grades 2-3) More complex plots, feeding imagination and growing information skills

For more information visit growandread.com.

Published by Fabled Films LLC, New York

ISBN: 978-1-944020-32-3

Library of Congress Control Number: 2019955039

First Edition: April 2020

1 3 5 7 9 10 8 6 4 2

Cover Designed by Jaime Mendola-Hobbie
Jacket & Interior Art by Josie Yee
Interior Book Design by Aleks Gulan
Typeset in Stemple Garamond, Mrs. Ant and Pacific Northwest
Printed by Everbest in China

FABLED FILMS PRESS
NEW YORK CITY
fabledfilms.com

For information on bulk purchases for promotional use please contact Consortium Book Sales & Distribution Sales department at ingrampublishersvcs@ingramcontent.com or 1-866-400-5351.

The
Best Burp

by

Tracey Hecht

Illustrations by
Josie Yee

Fabled Films Press
New York

Chapter 1

The sky was clear.

There were no clouds.

But Tobin heard a **rumble!**

"Is that thunder?" Tobin asked.

"Not thunder!"

Bismark said to Tobin.

"That was Bink's burp."

"The best burp of the night!"

Bink said.

"Bah!" Bismark said.

"That was not the best burp.

MY burp was better!"

"No, *MY* burp was better!"

Bink said.

"No, *MY* burp was better!"

Bismark said.

"I have an idea!" Bink said.

"Let's have a **burp-off!**"

Chapter 2

"A burp-off!" Bismark said.

"That's the best idea ever!

Tobin, you tell us which burp is bigger."

"Okay!" Tobin said. "On the count of three—

One," Tobin said.
Bismark took a deep breath.

"Two," Tobin said.
Bink took a deep breath.

"Three!"

Tobin called out.

RRP!

Bismark and Bink both let out

BIG burps!

Dawn popped her head over a bush.

"Who is making those **BIG** burps?"

the fox asked.

Chapter 3

Bismark pointed at Bink.

Bink pointed at Bismark.

But when Bismark pointed at Bink,

and Bink pointed at Bismark . . .

. . . it looked like they were blaming Tobin!

"But . . . !"

Tobin said. "It was not my burp-off.

Bismark and Bink are the ones to blame."

Dawn smiled.

"Burps are natural," Dawn said.

"But a burp-off?

And blaming each other?

Are those ways to be your best self?"

"No,"
Bismark said.

"Please excuse us,"
Bink said.

"We're sorry,"
Tobin added.

"Now that is much better!" Dawn said.

Dawn held a leaf over Tobin, Bismark, and Bink to keep them dry.

"Thank you!"

"Thank you!"

"Thank you!"

Tobin, Bismark, and Bink all said.

"And being your best self for your best friends . . ." Dawn said,

". . . now that is the best!"

The NOCTURNALS

FUN FACTS!

What Is a Nocturnal Animal?

Nocturnal
(NOK-tur-nel) *adjective*
Nocturnal animals are awake at night and sleep during the day.

The Nocturnal Animal Friends in the Story

Pangolin
(PANG-guh-lin) *noun*

Pangolins have small, hard plates on their bodies. They have long tongues but no teeth. They are shy, and they make a stinky smell or curl into a ball when they are scared. They live in Asia and Africa, but there are not many of them left in the world. Many people are trying to protect pangolins and the places where they live.

Red Fox
(RED FAHKS) *noun*

Red Foxes have yellow, orange, or red fur and black feet. Their big, bushy tails help to keep them warm. They have very strong ears. They can hear things that people cannot! They live in cozy dens with their parents when they are young. When they are grown-ups, they like to be alone. Foxes are very smart, and they like to play.

Sugar Glider

(SHOO-ger GLAHY-der) *noun*

Sugar Gliders have small bodies, big eyes, and gray fur. When they are babies, they ride around in a special pocket on their mothers' bellies. They like to eat fruit and other sweet plants. Sugar gliders like to live in groups in tree branches. They cannot fly, but they can stretch out their bodies and float like a leaf from tree to tree.

Bat

(Baat) *noun*

Bats are small animals that have fur and wings to help them fly. Most bats eat fruit and insects. An average bat can eat more than a thousand insects per hour. They have very good vision which helps them fly in the dark caves they call their home.

Grow & Read Storytime Activities
For The Nocturnals Early Reader Books!

Download Free Printables:

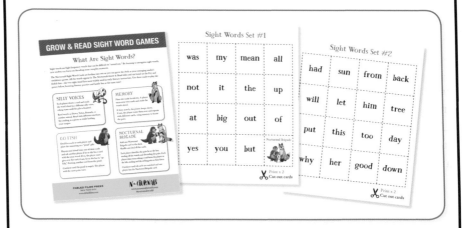

Sight Word Games

Brigade Mask Craft and Coloring Pages!

Visit **growandread.com**
#NocturnalsWorld

About the Author

Tracey Hecht is a writer and entrepreneur who has written, directed and produced for film. She created a Nocturnals Read Aloud Writing Program in partnership with the New York Public Library that has expanded nationwide. Tracey splits her time between Oquossoc, Maine and New York City.

About the Illustrator

Josie Yee is an award-winning illustrator and graphic artist specializing in children's publishing. She received her BFA from Arizona State University and studied Illustration at the Academy of Art University in San Francisco. She lives in New York City with her daughter, Ana, and their cat, Dude.

About Fabled Films & Fabled Films Press

Fabled Films is a publishing and entertainment company creating original content for young readers and middle grade audiences. Fabled Films Press combines strong literary properties with high quality production values to connect books with generations of parents and their children. Each property is supported by websites, educator guides and activities for bookstores, educators and librarians, as well as videos, social media content and supplemental entertainment for additional platforms.

fabledfilms.com

FABLED FILMS PRESS
NEW YORK CITY

Read All of The Grow & Read Nocturnal Brigade Adventures!

This series can help children enjoy learning to read and is perfect for shared reading and reading aloud.

Great For Kids Ages 5-7

Level 1

Level 2

Level 3

Visit nocturnalsworld.com to download fun nighttime activities
#NocturnalsWorld